WALT DISNEY PRODUCTIONS
presents

A Narrow Escape

Random House 🏠 New York

Book Club Edition

First American Edition. Copyright © 1984 by Walt Disney Productions. All rights reserved under International and Pan-American Copyright Conventions. Published in the United States by Random House, Inc., New York, and simultaneously in Canada by Random House of Canada Limited, Toronto. Originally published in Denmark as MIKKEL OG MILLE: RAËVEUNGERNE PAA OPDAGELSE by Gutenberghus Gruppen, Copenhagen. ISBN: 0-394-86537-5   Manufactured in the United States of America
4567890   ABCDEFGHIJK

One spring, two fox cubs were born.

Their father and mother were Tod and Vixey.

The cubs were named Tori and Tala.

The foxes lived in a game preserve.

Tori and Tala liked to play together.

At first they made sure to stay near Tod and Vixey.

Then the cubs grew bigger and bolder.

Tori and Tala began
to go exploring—but
not too far away!
They tried jumping
from a tree stump.

They tried crossing a stream on a log.
"You can do it, Tori!" said Tala.

They tried
to slide down
a steep bank.

But the cubs did not want to explore
a dark cave.

They were not THAT brave!

One day the cubs found a large log.
It was hollow inside.
"I dare you to run through it,"
Tala said to her brother.
Tori stepped inside the log.
It was very dark in there.

An angry badger lived in the log.
He growled and hissed at Tori.
Tori ran outside as fast as he could.
Tod and Vixey heard the noise.
They ran over to see what had happened.

"You must be more careful," Tod said
to the cubs. "Everyone is not a friend!"
"I think we must teach our children
about the world," said Vixey.

So the fox family began to take
long walks together.

"Many kinds of birds live near us,"
Tod said to Tori and Tala.

The foxes saw bobwhites and
pheasants in the grass.

A blue jay and a yellow warbler
sat in a tree.

A hawk soared in the sky.

There were larger animals too.
A deer was eating apples in an orchard.
A sleepy porcupine poked its head out
of a hole in a tree.

"Don't bother her!"
Vixey told the cubs.
"Her quills are sharp!"

Then Tod and Vixey took Tori and Tala
down to the stream.

"That raccoon is teaching her children
how to catch fish," said Tod.

The foxes ran past a woodchuck family.
The woodchucks were eating the roots
of wild carrots.

"Race you to the pond!" Tori called
to Tala.

A grasshopper hopped out of their way.

Tori reached the pond first.

"I'm going to catch that frog!"
Tori said. "Here I go!"
He jumped into the pond.

SPLASH!

The water was deep.
Tori could not swim.

"Help!" yelled Tori.
Tod jumped in to rescue the cub.

"You children must be careful!"
said Vixey. "Look before you leap.
The world is full of danger. And
the biggest danger of all is humans!"

Animals were safe in the game preserve.
Hunting was not allowed there.
But now it was time for the cubs
to learn about hunters.
So one day Tod and Vixey took Tori
and Tala outside the game preserve.

GAME PRESERVE
NO HUNTING

On the way, the cubs learned
how to escape from hunters.

"Run through water," said Tod. "Then
you won't leave a scent behind you."

The cubs learned how to run on walls
and fences.

"But run through the grass if a hunter
is close by," said Tod. "Then the hunter
won't see you."

Tod led his family to a farm.
It belonged to Mrs. Tweed.
"Most people will hurt foxes,"
said Tod. "But this lady is good.
She saved me from a hunter long ago."

Tod barked hello to Mrs. Tweed.

"Why, I do believe it's Tod!"
said Mrs. Tweed. "You're so big
now! And you have a family, too.
How nice of you to come by!"

The foxes ran back up the hill.
Mrs. Tweed waved good-bye.
"You be careful now, you hear?"
she called. "Amos Slade is around."

Amos Slade
lived nearby.

He was just
the man Tod
wanted to see.

Amos Slade was a hunter.

He owned two fierce hunting dogs—
Copper the hound and old Chief.

Right now everyone at Amos's place
was fast asleep.

Tod led the way up to the fence.

"See that man? He and his dogs
are dangerous," Tod whispered. "But
I was once friends with the hound."

"What happened?" asked Tala.

"Copper grew up and
learned to hunt foxes,"
Tod said sadly.

Copper was a very good hunting dog.

Copper could smell a fox
in his sleep.
And he smelled foxes now!
He woke up and growled.
Then he began to bark.

Amos Slade woke up
with a start.

Amos saw four foxtails beyond his fence.
"Foxes!" Amos yelled.
He grabbed his gun.
"Go get them, Copper!" Amos cried.
Copper chased after the foxes as fast
as he could.

"I bet those foxes ate every one
of my chickens!" said Amos.
He went over to his chicken coop.
It was empty!

"Come on, Chief!" Amos called. "Let's
go over to that Tweed woman's place.
That's where the foxes will go—
unless Copper got them first!"

Meanwhile, Copper
was following the scent
of the foxes.

Copper did not know
that he was tracking
his old friend Tod.

The cubs were too tired to run anymore.
So the foxes hid behind a wall.

Copper put his nose
over the wall.

"Hi! It's me!"
Tod said bravely.

"Tod! You'd better scram!" said Copper.
"Amos thinks you ate his chickens!"
"We never even SAW his chickens,"
said Tod.
"Get home and stay there!" said Copper.

So the foxes raced off.

Amos had arrived at Mrs. Tweed's farm.
Copper ran over to Amos and Chief.

"Where are those foxes?" Amos snarled
to Mrs. Tweed. "You must be hiding them!"
"What foxes?" asked Mrs. Tweed.

"The foxes that ate my chickens!"
said Amos. "Now hand them over!"
He did not notice Copper leaving.

Copper had smelled something he knew.
He followed his nose around the house
to Mrs. Tweed's garden.
There were Amos's chickens!
The chickens were pecking for worms
in the soft earth.

Copper barked.
Amos ran over.
"Did you find
the foxes, boy?"
the hunter said.

Amos went closer
to the garden....

"My chickens!" Amos said in surprise.
Mrs. Tweed appeared.

"What are those chickens doing here?"
Mrs. Tweed said. "I guess you never fixed
that hole in your fence. Your chickens
must have gotten out through the hole!"

"You should be ashamed of yourself, Amos!" said Mrs. Tweed. "Don't blame other people for your mistakes!"

"Well—um—let me get my car. I'll move the chickens out of your way," Amos said.

Amos headed for home.
And the fox family headed
for the game preserve.
But they were careful
not to leave tracks.
Amos's dogs might still
come after them!

The foxes reached home after dark.

"Whew-w! That was a narrow escape!"
said Tod.

"Too close for comfort," agreed Vixey.

"You were right," said Tala.
"The world is full of danger."
And Tori added, "But it can be
very exciting, too!"